• A FRANK ASCH BEAR BOOK •

PIZZA

• FRANK ASCH •

ALADDIN

New York   London   Toronto   Sydney   New Delhi

ALADDIN

An imprint of Simon & Schuster Children's Publishing Division

1230 Avenue of the Americas, New York, NY 10020

This Aladdin edition March 2015

For information about special discounts for bulk purchases,

please contact Simon & Schuster Special Sales at 1-866-506-1949

or business@simonandschuster.com.

The Simon & Schuster Speakers Bureau can bring authors to your live event.

For more information or to book an event contact the

Simon & Schuster Speakers Bureau at 1-866-248-3049

or visit our website at www.simonspeakers.com.

Designed by Karina Granda

The text of this book was set in Olympian LT Std.

Manufactured in the United States of America 0415 LAK

4 6 8 10 9 7 5 3

Library of Congress Cataloging-in-Publication Data

Asch, Frank, author, illustrator.

Pizza / Frank Asch.—First Aladdin hardcover edition.

pages cm—(A Frank Asch bear book)

Summary: After trying pizza for the very first time, everything Baby Bear sees reminds

him of the tasty treat and he decides never to eat anything else.

ISBN 978-1-4424-6675-3 (hc)

[1. Pizza—Fiction. 2. Bears—Fiction.] I. Title.

PZ7.A778Piz 2015

808.83'9362—dc23

2014026373

ISBN 978-1-4424-6677-7 (eBook)

One evening Papa Bear said, "Let's all go out
for dinner."

"Where shall we go?" asked Mama Bear.

"There's a new pizza parlor in town," replied
Papa Bear. "Let's eat there."

"Pizza? What's pizza?" asked Baby Bear.

"You've never had pizza before," said Papa Bear. "You're in for a treat!"

"But what if I don't like pizza?" asked Baby Bear. "Do I have to eat it anyway?"

"Don't worry, Dear," said Mama Bear. "You'll *like* pizza."

Baby Bear thought the pizza
parlor smelled nice.

The Bear family sat down at a small round table and ordered a large cheese pizza.

While they waited for their pizza to arrive, Baby Bear drew on the paper place mat with crayons.

Finally a waiter brought the pizza to
the table. "Nice and hot!" he said.

Then Papa Bear cut Baby Bear a slice of pizza.

"Let it cool for a while," said Mama Bear as she blew on Baby Bear's slice. "If you don't, you might burn your mouth."

When his slice of pizza was
cool enough, Baby Bear took
a big bite.

He had never tasted anything so yummy!

It was so *yummy*, Baby Bear felt like he was floating on a cloud! "Well?" asked Mama Bear. "Do you like pizza?"

"Like it?" cried Baby Bear. "I love it!"

On the way home, Baby Bear couldn't stop thinking about pizza.

He thought the moon looked like a big yellow pizza.

The wheels on all the cars he saw
looked like pizzas.

Even the manhole covers reminded him
of pizza.

That night as he lay fast asleep in his bed, Baby Bear dreamed that a giant pizza-shaped spaceship landed in his backyard.

In his dream, he went outside to investigate.

When the spaceship hatch opened, out marched three alien chefs.

One was from the planet Crouton.

"Try my macaroni and cheese pizza," he said.

"No! No!" said a chef from the Asparagus Galaxy.

"Try my peanut butter and jelly pizza!"

"Forget about their pizzas," said a third chef from a planet beyond the Lobster Nebula. "Try my chocolate chip pizza!"

Just then Papa Bear called, "Wake up, Baby
Bear, it's breakfast time!"

Baby Bear jumped out of bed, got dressed,
and ran downstairs.

"Good morning, Baby Bear!" said Mama Bear.

"Would you like some eggs for breakfast?"

"Er . . . No thanks," said Baby Bear.

"How about some nice, hot oatmeal?"
asked Papa Bear.

"Hmmm . . . Not this morning,"
answered Baby Bear.

"Fruit cup? Corn flakes?" asked Mama Bear.
"Sorry, not interested," said Baby Bear.

"French toast? Pancakes? Waffles?"
asked Mama and Papa Bear.
"No! No! No!" said Baby Bear.

"Then what do you want?" asked
Mama and Papa Bear.

"Silly Mama! Silly Papa!" cried Baby Bear.